A **Martha's Farm** STORY

Martha and the Picnic Party

by Steve Lavis

Ragged Bears Publishing

After a hard day working on the farm, Martha decided she was going to have a quiet picnic by the river. Jake licked his lips and wagged his tail, "Yes, you can come too," laughed Martha.

Jake bounced off to tell Scarecrow. "You lucky thing," said Scarecrow. "Picnic!" clucked the nosey chickens at the mention of food.

"Come on, Jake!" called Martha. With two wags of his tail, Jake was across the garden and jumping into the boat. "Careful Jake, or we'll both end up in the river!" said Martha.

The sun was shining, the river was sparkling. "Mmm, this is the life Jake, what a good day for a picnic," sighed Martha as she let the boat drift slowly down river.

"Cluck! Cluck! Cluck!"
The silence was broken. The silly
chickens had got themselves stuck!
"You had better come along with
Jake and me," said Martha helping
the chickens into the boat.

The sun was shining, the river was sparkling...

"Quack! Quack! Quack!"

Around the bend in the river came the ducks...

"We're going on a picnic!" clucked the chickens.
"Picnic!" quacked the greedy ducks and flapped up
into the boat.

It was a fine day for a picnic...

"Baa! Baa! Baa!"

Around the bend in the river was a sheep stuck in the muddy undergrowth.

SLURP! Martha pulled the sheep out of the mud and into the boat. So now Martha, Jake, five chickens, three ducks *and* a wet and muddy sheep all drifted under the bridge and down the river.

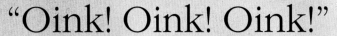

"Oink! Oink! Oink!"
On the next bend of the river bank was a pig. "That pig has escaped from somewhere," said Martha, and thinking quickly opened the picnic basket

Yum Yum!

and offered the pig a cake.

"Now let's see if we can find where you've come from," said Martha lifting the little pig into the boat.

"Oink! Oink!" grunted the pig nuzzling the picnic basket.

"Woof! Woof!" barked Jake.

"Cluck! Cluck!" clucked the chickens.

"Quack! Quack!" quacked the ducks.

"Baa! Baa!" bleated the sheep.

"SIT DOWN! KEEP STILL! You're all rocking the boat!" shouted Martha as the boat started to tip sideways.

"Help!" Martha jumped for the river-bank just as the boat tipped right over!

"Well, well, what have we here?" said Farmer Ted looking over the hedge from the neighbouring farm.

"Is this your pig, Ted?" asked Martha crossly, pointing at the little round pig who was sitting in the river, wondering what had just happened.

But Farmer Ted's pig and all the other animals soon cheered up when Martha opened the picnic basket

and shared out all the food. "So much for my *quiet* picnic by the river!" sighed Martha.

"When I've finished this bit of cake, I'll take you all home in my old Land Rover, and we can come back tomorrow and fetch your boat," suggested Ted.

The sun was starting to set and the river was turning into a silvery mirror. It had been a good day for a picnic, even if it hadn't turned out *quite* as Martha had expected!